No More Clowning Around!

The crowd erupted into cheers as Togo, the Crying Clown, stepped into the spotlight. He waved, then began juggling half a dozen cigar boxes.

Watching from backstage, Bert was fascinated. Time after time the whole stack of boxes seemed about to fall. And time after time Togo caught them at the very last moment.

A flicker of movement, just out of range of the spotlight, caught Bert's attention. He glanced up, then gasped.

One of the trapezes had come unfastened. It was starting to fall. Faster and faster it came.

And Togo was directly in its path!

Books in The New Bobbsey Twins series

Available from MINSTREL Books

THE NEW
Bobbsey Twins
#13
Twins

THE CASE OF THE CRYING CLOWN

LAURA LEE HOPE

ILLUSTRATED BY PAUL JENNIS

A MINSTREL® BOOK

PUBLISHED BY POCKET BOOKS

New York   London   Toronto   Sydney   Tokyo

A MINSTREL PAPERBACK *ORIGINAL*

A Minstrel Book published by
POCKET BOOKS, a division of Simon & Schuster Inc.
1230 Avenue of the Americas, New York, NY 10020

Copyright © 1989 by Simon & Schuster Inc.
Cover artwork copyright © 1989 by Linda Thomas
Produced by Mega-Books of New York, Inc.

ISBN: 0-671-55501-4

First Minstrel Books printing August 1989

10 9 8 7 6 5 4 3 2 1

THE NEW BOBBSEY TWINS is a trademark
of Simon & Schuster Inc.

THE BOBBSEY TWINS, A MINSTREL BOOK and colophon
are registered trademarks of Simon & Schuster Inc.

Printed in the U.S.A.

Contents

THE CASE OF THE CRYING CLOWN

1

Big Top Trouble

"Wow, look at that!" Flossie Bobbsey pointed at the man dancing down the circus midway. "He must be a zillion feet tall," she said.

It was true—the tall man's red- and white-striped trousers seemed to go on forever. He towered over the people around him. As he kicked his long legs high in the air, the crowd gasped and clapped.

"He can't be real, can he?" Flossie asked. "Nobody's that tall."

"He's wearing stilts," said twelve-year-old Bert Bobbsey. "You can see them when he kicks."

Freddie, Flossie's twin brother, stood on his tiptoes. His blue eyes were wide with wonder. "I see them," he said. "That's amazing. I'll bet it took him a long time to learn to walk on stilts that tall."

"Where?" Flossie pressed forward. "I can't see."

"Hey, watch out," her older sister, Nan, said sternly. "You just got your cotton candy in my hair." She brushed at the sticky stuff with her fingers.

"Gee, Nan, you look better with pink hair," Bert teased his twin. "Why don't you make the rest of it pink, too?"

"I like it brown, thanks." Nan glanced around. "Freddie, Flossie, stay close," she called. "The crowds are getting pretty thick. Remember, I have the tickets. If you get lost, you'll miss the show."

The Magic Max Circus had arrived in Lakeport the week before, but this was the first chance the twins had had to visit the circus. Richard Bobbsey, the twins' father, had just dropped them off at the entrance. The huge canvas tent and the colorful attractions of the midway had turned the town fairgrounds into a magical place.

Flossie sniffed the breeze. "Mmmm," she said. "Fresh-roasted peanuts! Nan, can I have some money?"

"Not a chance," Nan said. "Who just had a big lunch? *And* a cotton candy?"

"Only half a cotton candy," Flossie protested. "The rest ended up in your hair."

"Don't remind me. Hey, listen!"

From the far end of the midway came the lively sound of a brass band. It was drawing closer.

The musicians wore bright red uniforms with gold trim. Their brass instruments glittered in the afternoon sunlight. As the band marched through the crowd, everyone began to cheer.

"Look at that clown," Freddie yelled. "He's juggling!"

In front of the musicians a clown in a white suit with big gold pom-poms pedaled a unicycle. His one-wheeled cycle zigzagged down the midway, first forward, then backward, then forward and backward again. The clown's face was painted white. He wore a big red nose and a sad smile. Painted tears spilled down his cheeks.

What really excited Freddie, though, were the five long, slender wooden clubs that the clown threw into the air.

"Five clubs at once," Freddie said. "That must be Togo, the Crying Clown. I saw him on the news last night. He's practically the best juggler in the whole world. I wish I could juggle like Togo."

"Keep practicing," Bert teased.

"Come on, let's find our seats," Nan said. "It's almost time for the show to start."

Peggy the seal spun the big red-and-blue ball on her nose, then tossed it toward her partner, Bonzer. Bonzer let out a loud bark. He leaned forward, balanced on his flippers, and batted the ball with his tail. It soared high into the air. Peggy weaved her head back and forth, watching the ball. It was falling now, very fast.

Nan held her breath. Freddie, sitting next to her, grabbed her arm. "She's going to miss," he muttered. "I know she is."

"Shh!"

Suddenly the ball was spinning on the end of Peggy's nose again. The seal held her pose for a few moments, then tossed the ball to her trainer.

Freddie sprang up and shouted, "Yay!" The rest of the audience was clapping and cheering, too. Peggy and Bonzer waddled forward, bowed, and started to clap back.

Flossie turned to Bert with shining eyes. "Do seals make good pets?" she asked. "I think I want one."

"They are pretty cute," Bert replied. "But I don't know about keeping them as pets. You'd need to have a lot of room. And a swimming pool."

"And a lot of fish to feed them," Freddie added.

"But we have room," Flossie said. "We have a pool, too. That old plastic pool down in the cellar. We could put it out in the yard and fill it with water."

Bert grinned and shook his head. "I don't think Mom and Dad would be thrilled to keep a pet seal. Not to mention all those fish."

"Shh," said Freddie. "Here comes Togo. He's the best ever!"

As the crying clown walked into the center ring, he stared anxiously at the four hats he was juggling. A bright red one kept coming down almost out of his reach.

Freddie grabbed Nan's arm again. He was almost spilling out of his seat with the suspense. "He's going to trip," he said. "I know he is. Look out!"

As Togo stretched way out to catch the red hat, his foot caught on the edge of the ring. The audience gasped. Togo toppled forward. He was about to hit the sawdust-covered floor when, somehow, the fall turned into a somersault.

The clown ended up sitting cross-legged on

the ground with his arms spread wide. Just then, the first of the hats landed on his head. Two! Three! Four! The rest of the hats stacked themselves on top of the first one—and the red hat was on top.

When the cheering finally stopped, Freddie turned to Nan. His face was split with a grin of relief. "What did I tell you?" he said. "The best!"

At last came the grand finale parade, led by four elephants. Togo, the performing seals, and a team of trick riders called the Galloping Senters got the loudest cheers.

As the parade left the arena and the music died down, Flossie said, "What a great show! I loved everything. But I loved Togo best of all."

"Me, too," said Freddie. "I wish I could meet him. Maybe he'd teach me some new juggling tricks."

"He seemed really nice," Nan said. "What if we went out back and said hello?"

Freddie's eyes went as wide as saucers. "Do you think we could? Really?"

Bert grinned and clapped him on the shoulder. "Sure. At least, we could try. Let's go!"

The back part of the fairgrounds was a maze of tents, house trailers, and cars. The twins wandered around for a few minutes, then stopped in confusion.

"We'd better ask somebody," Bert said.

Nan looked around. A girl was coming up the path. She wore a baseball jacket over her spangled blue tights and sequined leotard.

"Hi," Nan said. "Aren't you one of the horse-back riders? You were terrific."

The girl blushed. "Thanks," she said. "I'm glad you liked the act."

Nan introduced herself and the rest of the Bobbseys. Then she explained that they wanted to meet Togo. "Do you think he'd mind?" she added.

"Oh, no," the girl said. "He loves to meet fans, especially kids. I'll show you where he lives."

She led them to a silver trailer and tapped at the door. Togo opened it. He had a towel tucked around his neck. Most of his face was still white, but he had wiped off the makeup around his eyes and had taken off his false nose. He looked as if he were wearing a mask.

"Hi, Sarah," he said. "You rode well today. Who are your friends?"

"Meet the Bobbseys," Sarah replied. "They wanted to tell you how much they liked your act."

"Really?" Togo gave them a big, warm smile. "Wonderful! Would you like to come in and watch me take off my face?" The twins and Sarah followed Togo into the trailer. He sat down in front of a big mirror and started smearing cream on his cheeks and forehead. As he wiped off the cream, he asked, "Are all of you brothers and sisters?"

"Uh-huh," Nan said. "Bert and I are twins, and so are Flossie and Freddie."

Freddie edged forward. "Mr. Togo?" he said. "I'm learning how to juggle."

"Are you, Freddie?" the clown replied. "That's great! I started when I was about your age. Will you show me later?"

Freddie nodded. His face was bright red.

Flossie tugged at Togo's sleeve.

The clown looked at her, but before he could speak, there was a loud knock at the door. "Come in," he called.

The door opened and a voice said, "Excuse me, sir, but does the blue car outside belong to you?"

Nan started as she recognized the voice of Lieutenant Pike of the Lakeport police. What did he want here at the circus?

"That's right," Togo said. "Why?"

Lieutenant Pike came inside. His eyes widened when he saw the Bobbseys. "That car has been noticed at the scene of several burglaries this week," he explained. "Do you mind if I take a look around?"

"Burglaries!" The clown seemed stunned. "No, of course not. Look all you like."

The Bobbseys and their new friend Sarah exchanged concerned looks. Lieutenant Pike called to a police officer to come inside. The lieutenant looked around the room, then walked down the hall to another room. The officer waited with his back to the door.

Togo went back to cleaning off his makeup. Nan noticed that he kept wiping at the same spot on his cheek.

Lieutenant Pike came back carrying a pillowcase. Whatever was in it clinked. "The silver tea set in here matches the description of one that was stolen yesterday," he said. "Can you explain what it was doing in your bedroom?"

Togo shook his head. "No. I never saw that pillowcase before," he said. "And I don't even drink tea."

"I see." Lieutenant Pike handed the pillowcase to the police officer and walked over to stand next to Togo. "I'm sorry, sir," he said to the clown. "You'll have to come along with me. You're under arrest!"

2

Arrest That Clown!

"They're arresting the wrong person," Sarah said to the twins. "I *know* Togo's innocent." She brushed angry tears from her eyes. "He's the sweetest, kindest person in the world. He could never be a burglar."

The police car pulled away, with Togo in it. The clown turned his head for a moment and looked at the children. Then he looked straight ahead. His face, without its makeup now, was still very sad.

"Listen, Sarah," Bert said. "Maybe we can help clear Togo. We've done a lot of detective work."

"For real?" She stared at Bert, then at Nan.

"Sure," Nan said. "We know Lieutenant Pike

from cases we've worked on. And he knows us."

"And we've got a jump on him," added Freddie. "Because we know Togo's innocent and he doesn't."

"Well, if you really think you can help . . . Come on, let's go see Max—Max Morrison. He owns the circus."

"You mean Magic Max?" asked Flossie. "Is he really magic?"

Sarah laughed. "Not as far as I know, but he's a nice man. Come on. The office trailer is just down this way."

As soon as he saw Max, Freddie recognized him as the ringmaster for the show. Without his polished boots, white riding breeches, red coat with navy blue stripes, and shiny top hat, Max looked very ordinary. Ordinary and worried.

When the twins walked in, Max was talking to a man with a bushy mustache, who was sitting behind a desk. Max looked up, saw Sarah, and gave her a big smile. "It's my favorite rider," he said. Then he looked at her more closely. "Why, what's the matter?"

"Someone came and arrested Togo," Sarah said. "They took him away in a police car."

Bert and Nan quickly filled in the details Sarah had left out.

"Ridiculous," Max said loudly. "I'll go downtown and straighten this out right now. Bob," he added, turning to the man at the desk, "you take care of those ticket reservations while I'm gone, okay?"

The other man nodded without looking up.

Sarah and the twins followed Max out of the office. Outside, Freddie stopped for a moment and took three soft sponge balls from his pants pocket. He had just remembered how Togo had done one of his juggling tricks. It had looked pretty easy when Togo did it, but Freddie had a hunch that didn't mean much.

He tossed the sponge balls into the air and tried to do the funny wrist turn that was most of the trick. He was starting to think that he was getting the hang of it when somebody bumped into him from behind. Freddie staggered and almost fell, and the sponge balls went in three different directions.

"Hey, why don't you—" he began, but the man who had jostled him was far ahead, almost running after Max. Freddie collected the balls and went after him.

"No lead clown and the whole show falls down," the man was saying as Freddie came within hearing.

Freddie stared up at his face. The man was

starting to look familiar. Wasn't he the clown who had followed Togo around the ring during Togo's act, doing everything he could to mess Togo up?

"Sorry, Sunny," Max replied. "I don't think you're ready. Tell you what—if I can't get Togo back in time for the eight o'clock show, maybe we'll expand your number a little. Okay?"

"No, it's not!" The man whirled around and stormed off. He didn't even seem to see Freddie, and he bumped into him again, hard enough to send Freddie sprawling in the dust.

Max helped Freddie to his feet. "Are you all right, son?" he asked. "Sunny is a little quick to fly off the handle sometimes."

"He bumped into me twice," Freddie said. "That's not very nice."

"No, it isn't." The circus owner brushed the dust from Freddie's back. "You'll be all right. See you later."

Freddie caught up to the others and told them about Sunny's conversation with Max. "What I want to know," Freddie concluded, "is how Sunny already knew about Togo getting arrested."

Sarah shrugged her shoulders. "Word gets around fast in a circus," she said. "It's like one big family."

THE CASE OF THE CRYING CLOWN

"Yeah, maybe," Freddie said. He wasn't convinced.

Bert was standing with his hands in his pockets, staring down at the ground. After a moment he said, "If Togo isn't the burglar—"

Sarah whirled around to face him. "Of course he isn't!" she declared.

"Okay," Bert said. "But if—since—he isn't, who is? That loot didn't walk into his trailer. Somebody put it there."

"And whoever it was is the real crook," Flossie said.

"Sure!" Freddie was hopping from one foot to the other with excitement. "He was trying to frame Togo, to get him arrested!"

"But nobody would do a thing like that," said Sarah. "Togo is the nicest person in the whole show. Everyone's his friend. Anybody who needs help always asks him first, because he's sure to give it. Why, look at the way everybody borrows his car. A lot of times they don't even bother to ask him, because he always says yes."

"He does?" Bert asked. He looked at Nan and raised his eyebrows. She gave him a thoughtful nod in return.

The twins followed Sarah up the path in the direction of the big top.

"Hey, look!" Flossie said suddenly. "Isn't that Togo's trailer? The door isn't closed."

"Maybe the police came back," Sarah said.

Bert looked up and down the path. "There's no police car nearby," he pointed out. "I wonder . . ."

He walked over and rapped loudly on the door of the trailer. "Is anybody in there?" he called.

There was no answer. Bert thought he heard a noise from inside. It sounded like somebody walking very carefully. A moment later Bert was sure he heard a faint click.

"You guys wait here," he said, and slipped through the door.

Bert's heart was pounding loudly as he looked around the living room. No one was in sight, and nothing seemed to be out of place. Even the dressing table looked fairly neat.

The short, narrow hallway that led between the tiny kitchen and an even tinier closet to the bedroom was empty. The bedroom door was closed.

Bert frowned and tried to think back. Hadn't that door been open before?

Sure! As they were leaving the trailer earlier, he had glanced back and noticed the view through the doorway. Someone must have closed the door since then. Whoever it was might still be in the bedroom.

Bert tiptoed down the hallway, wiped his palm on his pants leg, and reached for the door-knob.

He held his breath and started to open the door, then froze. What was that rustling noise? Where was it coming from? The bedroom? No, it was behind him. Was somebody hiding in the kitchen?

He started to turn. Suddenly the closet door was flung open. Bert tried to duck back, but the door slammed into him and knocked him to the floor!

3

Mysterious Footprints

Bert pushed himself up onto his hands and knees. He felt dizzy, and his ears were ringing. He lurched to his feet and reached up to feel the bump on his forehead. It hurt.

The door of the trailer was just a few feet away. He staggered over and leaned out.

Nan saw him first. "Bert, are you all right?" she demanded. "What happened?"

"A closet door knocked me down," he said. "Did he come out this way?"

"Who?" asked Flossie.

"I don't know. I didn't see anyone."

"Oh. Well, nobody came out this way."

"The other side!" Freddie shouted, and made a dash for the back of the trailer. Nan, Sarah, and Flossie were close behind him. Bert tried to run, too, but every step made his head ache.

"What did you see?" Nan was asking Freddie as Bert caught up to them.

"Nothing," Freddie replied. "I just figured that if the crook didn't come out the door, he had to have come out on this side. And he did, too. Look!"

The window Freddie was pointing to had been flung all the way open. Its screen was dangling from one hinge. The screen bulged as if somebody had kicked it.

Sarah started toward the window, but Bert grabbed her arm.

"Wait," he said. "I think I see some important evidence."

The ground under the window was soft and damp. Bert knelt down, took out the Rex Sleuther pocket tool he always carried, and pulled out the tape measure. He held it against two of the many footprints in the dirt.

"Why are those so important?" Sarah asked. "What about all the others?"

"All these prints show that lots of people go back and forth past here," Bert explained. "But these are the only prints that go sideways. They're deeper than the others, too. That means they were probably made by somebody

who jumped down from the window. Hey, that's funny . . ."

"What is?" asked Nan. "Did you find something?"

Bert frowned. "I don't know. Maybe. The print of the right foot is almost a quarter of an inch deeper than the one of the left foot. I wonder why?"

"Maybe he just landed funny," said Freddie. "With more of his weight on one foot."

"Maybe," Bert said again, nodding slowly. "Or, maybe . . . Oh, never mind."

He got to his feet and looked up and down the line of trailers.

"It makes me mad to think I was that close to the guy and I didn't even see his face," Bert said. Then he caught a glimpse of his watch. "Hey, we'd better get moving. Mom and Dad will be expecting us home pretty soon, you know."

"Sarah said we can have dinner with her," Flossie told Bert.

"Yeah, in the circus mess tent, with all the performers," Freddie added. "And afterward she'll take us to watch tonight's show from backstage."

"Can we, Bert? Can we, Nan?" pleaded Flossie. "Pretty please?"

Bert caught his twin sister's eye, then grinned. "We're on a case, aren't we?" he said. "And we can't investigate if we aren't here. If it's okay with Mom and Dad, I think it's a great idea."

Sarah led them to a phone, and Bert called home. Mrs. Bobbsey agreed to let them stay at the circus for dinner but said that she would pick up Flossie and Freddie right afterward. They had already had an exciting day, and going to the evening show would keep them out much too late. This news didn't make the younger twins very happy, but Bert and Nan promised to tell them about everything they missed.

Nan looked around the dining tent and listened to the hubbub of conversations. Bert was sitting across the table from her, talking to Sarah's father and mother. Freddie and Flossie were sitting on either side of Sarah's older brother. He was telling them about some of his circus adventures.

Nan turned to Sarah, who was sitting next to her. "Do all the people in the circus eat together all the time?" she asked.

Sarah laughed. "Oh, no," she replied. "Lots of times we fix our own meals and eat in our trailers. But when we're doing two shows a day, there's not enough time for that. It's simpler to let the mess crew do all the cooking and cleanup."

Nan was about to ask what it was like, moving from town to town and performing for new audiences every day, when a silence fell. She looked up. Max, the circus owner, was standing in the entrance. He stepped to one side, and she saw that Togo was right in back of him, smiling shyly.

Everyone started clapping and cheering. *Almost* everyone. The clown called Sunny was eating at a nearby table. He didn't look very sunny just then. In fact, his face was so stormy that Nan half expected to see lightning shoot out of his ears.

Max passed close to Nan's table, and Sarah's father, Louis Senter, called him over. They spoke quietly, but Nan heard every word.

"He is free, then?" Sarah's father began.

Max scowled. "Yes and no. The police had to let him go, because there is no hard evidence against him. But I'm sure they still think he's the guy they're after. It didn't help that he wouldn't tell them where he's been and what he's been doing since we got to Lakeport."

Nan glanced over at Sarah, to see what she

thought of this news. But Sarah was busy talking to Bert and didn't seem to have heard.

Sarah's dad looked startled. "You don't think Togo's guilty!"

"All I think is that he's keeping something secret from the police. And from me," Max said.

"Speaking of secrets—" Sarah's father stopped talking and glanced around. Nan looked down at her plate and hoped she wasn't blushing. "Speaking of secrets, is the eagle going to scream on Friday?"

The circus owner waved his hand in front of his face, as if he were chasing away a fly. "You tell me," he said. "I don't get it, Louis. We're pulling good houses, but the ducats aren't where they should be. If this keeps up, we may have to fold the top and turn civilian."

"That bad?" Sarah's father shook his head. Max patted him on the shoulder and walked away, leaving Nan to wonder what on earth they had been talking about.

After dinner, Sarah took the Bobbseys across the fairgrounds to the entrance, where Mrs. Bobbsey was going to pick up Freddie and Flossie.

Nan walked beside Sarah. In a quiet moment, she asked, "Sarah? What's a *ducat?*"

Sarah laughed. "It's an old circus word for money."

"And what does it mean when the eagle screams?"

Her new friend looked over at her. "It means it's payday," Sarah explained. "Where did you hear that?"

"Some men at dinner were talking," Nan said. "One of them said he might have to turn civilian."

"Oh, I hope not!" Sarah sounded shocked. "That means leaving the circus for good. No real circus people ever do that if they can help it. Who was it?"

Nan pretended not to hear the question. She would have to pass this important clue to Bert the first chance she got.

"I'm glad that Togo is free," she said to Sarah.

"So am I. The Magic Max Circus wouldn't be the same without him."

When Mrs. Bobbsey came to take Flossie and Freddie home, Sarah led Nan and Bert to the performers' entrance to the big top. An elderly man looked up from his magazine. "Evening, Sarah," he said.

"Hi, Ben," Sarah replied. "These are my friends the Bobbseys. They're doing some special work for Max. Will you please pass them in and out whenever they like?"

Ben gave the little group a curious look, but all he said was, "Sure thing, Sarah. You kids enjoy the show."

Backstage, Bert joined in the loud applause for the trapeze act performed by the Flying Maraskins. A moment later, as stagehands hoisted the trapezes up out of the way, the Maraskins themselves came out of the arena right past him. Under their makeup, they looked tired, but they smiled when he gave them a special cheer.

It was different, watching the show from backstage. It made Bert see that circus performers were not just glittering figures out of a storybook but real people. Who would have thought that a famous clown like Togo would stop on his way into the arena to say hello to Bert and Nan? But that was just what he had done.

The crowd erupted into cheers as Togo stepped into the spotlight. Some of them started chanting, "To-go, To-go, To-go!" He waved and held up his hands for silence, then began juggling what looked like half a dozen cigar boxes.

Bert was fascinated. He had never imagined that anyone could make a few simple boxes fly against gravity in so many different ways. Time after time the whole stack of boxes seemed about to fall. And time after time Togo caught them at the very last moment.

A flicker of movement, just out of range of the spotlight, distracted Bert and caught his attention. He glanced around, then upward. Suddenly he gasped. One of the trapezes had somehow come unfastened. It was starting to fall. Faster and faster it came. Its downward path would bring it sweeping across the arena just a few feet above the floor.

And Togo was directly in its path!

4

A Suspect Appears

As Nan watched Togo juggle his boxes, her mind kept returning to the conversation she had overheard between Max and Sarah's father. It could have meant only one thing. The circus was missing some of the money from ticket sales, so much that Max wasn't sure whether he could pay the performers and other employees that week. Money was missing, and a star of the circus was accused of a string of burglaries. Was there a connection?

A man in a long, black cloak with a high, stiff collar was standing right next to the trapeze rigging. Nan gave him a curious glance. Was he waiting to go on? She couldn't imagine how a Dracula look-alike would fit with Togo, but maybe he was part of the next act.

At that moment, Bert let out a gasp. Startled, Nan looked at him, then followed the direction of his eyes. One of the trapezes was swinging directly at the back of Togo's head.

Nan screamed.

Togo looked around. He saw his danger at once. Throwing the boxes into the air, he flung himself to the side and began a spectacular series of cartwheels that took him halfway across the arena. Just as he finished with a flip, the runaway trapeze struck one of the cigar boxes and turned it into splinters.

The crowd cheered. They seemed to think that the sudden cartwheels were part of Togo's act. Nan knew better. The clown had come very close to being badly hurt.

Max was standing nearby, watching the end of Togo's act. His face was pale. When one of the crew walked past, Max grabbed his arm. "Who's responsible for the trapeze rigging?" he demanded.

The stagehand was pale, too. "That'd be Artie," he replied. "But—"

"Get him over here. Now."

A few moments later a tall, burly man walked up. He didn't give the circus owner time to say a word.

"I fastened those lines myself," he said. "No way one of them could have worked loose, no way at all."

"One of them did," Max replied. "You saw, didn't you?"

"Yes, sir, I saw. But I'm telling you, it couldn't have worked loose. No way!"

"Mr. Max?" Nan said. "Right before the trapeze fell, I saw somebody in a long, black cape standing next to the ropes."

"Did you, sweetheart?" Max studied her face for a moment, then nodded. "I guess you did. Long, black cape—who could that be? There are no capes in the show just now. We'd better have a look around."

He turned to the stagehand. "Artie, you and the other guys, whoever's free, take a good look around. Look for a black cape or anything else that doesn't belong."

"We'll look around, too," Nan said, and dragged Bert away before the circus owner could tell them not to.

As soon as they were out of hearing range, Nan turned to Bert and asked, "Where would you hide a black cape if you were in a big hurry?"

Bert tugged at his earlobe. "I don't know— someplace black?"

"That's what I thought, too. Someplace like—" She looked around and noticed the black curtains in back of the bandstand. "There!"

They hurried over and began pulling and tugging at the curtains. The dust made Bert sneeze. They were near the end of the row of curtains when Nan said, "I knew it!"

She bent down and picked up a long, heavy black cloak and showed it to Bert.

"What's that white stuff?" he asked.

"It looks like clown makeup, doesn't it?" Nan replied. "Let's bring the cape over to Max."

The circus owner was standing near the performers' entrance. He looked at the cloak, sniffed the collar, and sent someone to find Sunny.

"Were you wearing this a little while ago?" Max asked when Sunny showed up.

The Bobbseys moved closer to hear the clown's answer.

Sunny looked around, shifted his weight from one foot to the other, and finally said, "Sure. I wanted to watch Togo's number, and I didn't want my costume to be distracting, so I covered it up."

"Where did you watch from?"

"I don't know, over there somewhere." He waved his hand in the direction of the arena. "Why?"

"I hear you were right next to the trapeze rigging," Max said. "Just before that line came loose."

"Now, wait a minute—" Sunny looked around again, as if he were planning to run.

Max put his hand on the clown's shoulder. "What if I tell you somebody saw you fiddling with that rope? Togo has a lot of friends, you know."

"I didn't mean to do anything," Sunny said. "I was leaning back, and I guess my hand was on the rope. All of a sudden it came loose, I don't know how. When I saw what had happened, I knew nobody would believe me, so I hid that cape and kept my mouth shut. You believe me, don't you?"

Max looked at him with narrowed eyes. At last he said, "I don't know if I do or not, Sunny. But if there are any more 'accidents,' you'd better not be anywhere around."

"What do we do this morning?" Freddie asked.

"Yeah, we want to help," added Flossie. "We missed all the excitement last night."

Nan finished pouring milk on her cereal, then tapped the stack of newspapers next to her bowl. "I've been going through the *Lakeport News* and making a list of burglaries," she said. "I think we need to talk to the people who got robbed."

"What if we split up in teams and each take half of the list?" Bert suggested. "That way we'll be done twice as fast."

"Good idea," said Nan. "Flossie, why don't you come with me?"

After breakfast the twins divided up the names and got on their bikes. The first house Nan and Flossie went to was dark and silent, but at the second one, a man smoking a pipe answered the door.

"We're doing a school project on crime in our neighborhood," Nan explained. "And we saw in the paper that you were robbed the other day."

The man's face turned red. "I sure was," he said. "A fine thing, you take your family out to have a nice time, you come home, and what do you find? Someone's broken in and stolen your VCR!"

"You were all away when it happened?" asked Nan.

"Yes, we were all at the circus."

Nan met Flossie's eyes and frowned. "The Magic Max Circus?"

"Sure, it's our favorite. We always order our tickets way in advance, just to be sure we don't miss it."

"When did the burglary happen? In the middle of the evening? Were any lights on in the house?"

"Oh, yes. We always leave a few lights on when we go out at night. It makes us feel safer. Ha! A lot of good it did this time!"

Flossie stepped back and looked up at the house. "How did the burglar get in?" she asked.

"That's another thing," the man replied. "Whenever we go out, we always close and lock all the windows on the first floor. The burglar must have climbed up on the back porch and jumped across to our bedroom window. I wouldn't like to try it myself—I'd probably fall and break my neck."

"Can we see where the burglar got in?" asked Nan.

"Why not?" The man led them around the house to the backyard and pointed to the bedroom window. The narrow windowsill was at least six feet away from the edge of the porch roof.

"Some jump," Nan said. "Well, thanks for talking to us."

"No problem," the man replied as he let them out of the yard.

Flossie and Nan went on to the third house on their list. The woman who came to the door didn't have time to talk. She did tell them that the burglar had climbed in through a second-floor window and that she and her husband had been at the circus at the time.

Nan said, "Did you order your tickets ahead of time?"

"Why, yes, we did," the woman replied. "As a rule we buy them at the gate, but we wanted to be sure to get in. It was my husband's birthday."

The girls stopped at a playground on the way home and sat on the merry-go-round.

"You can't miss it," Nan said. "The burglar has to be connected with the Magic Max Circus."

Flossie's face crumpled up, as if she were about to burst into tears. "You mean Lieutenant Pike is right?" she said. "I can't believe it. I *won't* believe it. That dear, sweet Togo is not a crook. He's not, he's *not!*"

5

Juggling the Clues

"Were the people on your list at the circus when their houses were robbed?" asked Nan. She, Flossie, and Bert were sitting on the grass in their backyard. Freddie was standing up, practicing his juggling.

"Two of them were," Bert reported. "And both times the robber got in through an upstairs window. In the third robbery, somebody broke in through the kitchen door in the middle of the day. It sounded to me like it might have been a different burglar."

"Hmm," said Nan. "The ones who were at the circus—do you know how they bought their tickets? Did they order them in advance?"

Bert shook his head. "We didn't ask. Do you think that's an important clue?"

"I don't know. It might be."

One of Freddie's sponge practice balls got away from him. It soared up and came down squarely on Nan's nose.

"Will you please stop that?" she said. "It's hard enough to think without you bonking me on the head."

She tossed the ball back to Freddie, who caught it and stuffed it in his pants pocket with the others.

"You know what I think?" he said. "I think the burglar is really Sunny. It's all part of a plot to get Togo fired so Sunny can take over his job."

"Come on," said Flossie. "I *know* Togo isn't guilty, but do you really think Sunny would break into a bunch of houses, just to frame him?"

"Who else?" Freddie said. "According to Nan, it's somebody at the circus, right?"

"Maybe it's Max," Bert said. "We know that he's having money troubles. Maybe he decided to solve them by robbing houses."

Freddie shook his head. "It can't be him," he said. "He doesn't look like a burglar."

"You think they all wear striped shirts and little masks, like they do in the comics?" Bert said.

Nan raised her hands. "Hold on a minute. What we really need is more information."

Richard Bobbsey stepped out the back door and said, "What you really need is some lunch. And what I need is some volunteers. Whose turn is it to set the table?"

After lunch the Bobbseys biked over to the fairgrounds. As they approached the midway, Sarah came riding up on her pony. Instead of a sequined leotard, she was wearing faded jeans and a T-shirt.

"Hi," she called. "Detecting?"

"We hope so," Nan replied.

Sarah leaned forward and patted her pony's neck. "Good. Because somebody got into the office trailer last night and took a lot of money."

"Really?" Bert said. "Do the police have any suspects?"

"They don't know about it. I heard Max tell my dad that he wasn't going to tell them."

"What's your pony's name?" asked Flossie. She reached up to stroke its nose, but the pony reared back and gave a loud snort.

"This is Twist," Sarah said. "He's crazy about apples. I'll give you one later to feed to him."

"Really? Wow!"

"What about me?" demanded Freddie.

"You can feed him one, too. I've got a whole basket full of them."

Bert frowned. "Never mind the apples," he said. "What about this break-in? Why isn't Max going to report it to the police?"

Sarah hesitated, then said in a low voice, "Because it wasn't a break-in. Whoever stole the money knew how to get into the trailer. And Max had new locks put in just a day or two ago. You see what that means?"

"It had to be an inside job," said Nan.

"Um-hm. And we don't need any more bad publicity. People might start to think the show is jinxed and decide not to come see us."

"That's not fair," Flossie said. "It's not your fault if somebody's a crook."

"I know," Sarah replied. "But that's the way it is, just the same."

After a short silence, Bert said, "Maybe we'd better split up. I want to talk to Togo."

"And I want to talk to Max," said Nan.

"Freddie and Flossie can come with me," Sarah said. "We can meet some of the other people in the show and look for clues."

"Can we meet Peggy and Bonzer?" Freddie asked.

Sarah grinned. "The seals? Sure, why not?

But good luck if you think they'll answer your questions."

Bert finally found Togo in the big top. The clown was rehearsing his hat-juggling somersault. When Bert came into the arena, he stood up, tilted his head to the right, and let the four brightly colored hats tumble into his hand.

"That's wonderful," Bert said. "It's like magic!"

"Magic?" the clown replied. "I wish it were! I spent two years developing that bit, and I hardly ever use it."

"That's too bad. Can I ask you about your car?"

Togo's face brightened. "My car? Sure! Do you want to buy it?"

"No, I—"

"Will you take it as a gift?"

"No, it's just—"

"I didn't think so," said Togo. His face became so terribly sad that Bert wanted to reach over and pat him on the shoulder. Then the clown smiled and winked. "Never mind," he said. "What do you want to know?"

Bert asked the first of the questions he had planned to ask. "I hear you let people borrow your car a lot. Is that so?"

Togo sighed. "I used to," he said. "I even

used to leave the keys in the car's ashtray. That way, if anybody needed to use the car, the person wouldn't have to hunt for me first."

"So the burglar could have used it without you even knowing about it."

"I guess so," Togo said. "That's what I tried to explain to the police yesterday. They told me I should take better care of my property."

He reached into his pocket and pulled out a bunch of keys on a ring. "So from now on, anybody who wants to borrow my car will have to ask me first. It's only sensible, isn't it? And businesslike."

The terribly sad expression returned. "But you know?" the Crying Clown concluded. "I liked it better the other way. It was friendlier."

Once again a smile broke through. "Watch this," Togo commanded.

He took one of the hats and tossed it into the air. A moment later it landed with a *plop!* on Bert's head.

"Wow!" said Bert. He reached up and removed the hat.

"Not bad, huh?" Togo replied. "Want to join the circus?"

While Bert was talking to Togo, Nan walked across the lot to the office trailer and knocked on the door.

"Come in," Max called. When Nan opened the door, he added, "Hey, good work last night, finding that cape. You put a real scare into Sunny. He needed it."

"I heard you had more trouble last night," said Nan. "A robbery?"

Max narrowed his eyes. "Where'd you hear that? Never mind, I can guess. No comment."

"What about the burglary charges against Togo?" she continued. "Do you think you can get them dropped?"

"No comment," Max repeated.

Nan wrinkled her nose. "Is there anything you *will* comment on?"

The circus owner hesitated, then said, "No comment."

Nan decided to try a different kind of question. "Do a lot of people order tickets in advance, by mail?"

"Fewer and fewer," Max replied. "These days people mostly either telephone or just show up and trust that they'll get a seat."

He rummaged around on the desk. "Here, look," he said, handing Nan a sheet of paper. "That is all the advance sales for Lakeport. One page—a few years ago, it would have been seven or eight."

The telephone rang. He turned around to

answer it. Nan studied the paper in her hand, then held it up to the light. She recognized some of the names, from her list of burglary victims, but the rest—

Her heart started to pound. The name of the man she had talked to that morning had a faint scratch under it, as if from a fingernail. So did the names of the other burglary victims. There were also a couple of other names with scratches underneath, names she didn't recognize. She studied them. One had ordered tickets for the next night, and the other had bought four box seats for the early show that very evening.

Nan quickly scribbled down the name and address of the person holding tickets for that evening's performance. If her hunch was right, that family had an unexpected date with a burglar—and the burglar had an unexpected date with the Bobbsey twins!

6

Freddie's Narrow Escape

"Hey, kid! What do you think you're doing?"

Nan quickly dropped the sheet of paper on Max's desk and turned around. A man with a bushy mustache was standing in the doorway, glaring at her. She remembered seeing him in the office the day before. Had he noticed that she had been reading the list of advance-ticket buyers?

"It's all right, Bob," Max said, covering the mouthpiece of the telephone with his hand. "That's Nan, one of our local kid detectives. You remember, I told you about them."

"Oh, sure. Okay." Bob limped across the trailer to his desk and sat down. "I guess I'm a little edgy."

Max finished his phone call. "I thought you'd be back earlier," he said, turning to Bob.

"Sorry," Bob said. "I was picking up my motorbike at the garage. The guy said he'd fixed it, but the way it's running, I could have gotten back faster by walking."

"Maybe it's time for a new one," Max said. "Listen, I've been thinking. After last night, we need to do something about the way we handle the box-office cash. We can't afford to lose another day's receipts. What do you think about—"

"Later," Bob said quickly. He frowned and nodded his head in Nan's direction. He obviously didn't want Max to talk in front of her.

"Oh, come on," Max began, but Nan interrupted him.

"I have to go now," she announced. She gave the two men her brightest smile. "Have a nice day."

As she walked back along the lane, she could hear the brass band playing in the distance. The aroma of hot dogs and popcorn drifted over from the midway, making her stomach growl. "Be quiet!" she muttered.

Nan found Flossie and Freddie with Sarah, near the menagerie tent.

"Hi," Flossie said. "Isn't Bert with you?"

Nan shook her head. "He's off somewhere investigating on his own," she said. She stood with the others and watched Carlo Cortese, the animal tamer, move his lions from their enclosure to a traveling cage hitched to a pickup truck.

"They're beautiful," Flossie said.

"And big," added Freddie.

One of the lions turned its head and looked at them with sleepy eyes. Then it opened its mouth wide and let out a roar. Everyone ducked back, even Sarah.

The animal tamer smiled. "He's telling you 'hello,' " he said. He shut the cage door and got into the truck.

"It sounded more like 'bye-bye' to me," Freddie muttered as the truck moved away.

"Well, I don't care," said Flossie. "I think they're very sweet, and I don't think it's fair to keep them shut up in cages. How would you feel if you had to live in a cage all the time?"

It sounded to Nan as if she had just walked in on the middle of a long discussion.

"I wouldn't like it," Sarah replied. "But here they get fed and taken care of. They're really Carlo's pets."

"They're a little too big to curl up on his lap," Freddie said with a grin.

Sarah smiled back. "Sure, but they love it when he pets them and scratches behind their ears. You should hear them purr."

"Just think of listening to lions purr," said Nan. "Life in the circus really is different, isn't it?"

"Of course it is," Sarah said. "As I said before, once you're part of it, the circus is like a big family. Everybody looks out for everybody else. Like . . . Did you notice Bob Sawyer, Max's assistant?"

"The guy with the bushy mustache?"

"That's him. He used to be part of a high-wire act. They were good, too. But last year he and his partner had an accident, a bad fall."

"How terrible!" Flossie exclaimed.

Sarah shuddered. "It *was* terrible. I saw it happen. They both had to go to the hospital, and when Bob came out, he had a permanent limp. He'll never walk a tightrope again, but he's still part of the circus."

"What about his partner?" asked Nan.

"Cindy? She was hurt worse than Bob was. She's been in the hospital for almost a year. My dad says that she'll be getting out pretty soon. I hope so. She's really nice and I miss her."

"Will she come back to the circus?"

"Oh, sure," Sarah said. "Max will find something for her to do. That's what he did for Bob. Bob didn't really know anything about working in an office, but that didn't matter. He needed a job, so Max made up one for him. Paying for Cindy's doctors and care cost Bob a fortune. He even had to sell his car and trailer, and bunk in with the crew."

"Did he—" Nan began, but Freddie grabbed her arm.

"Hey," he said in a low voice, "I just saw that guy Sunny go by."

"So what?" Nan said.

"Shh. Not so loud! I don't think he saw us. He had a very sneaky look. I'll bet he's up to something. I'm going to follow him."

Freddie ran after the clown, making as little noise as he could. Nan called Freddie's name, but he ignored her. He didn't have time to stop and argue. If he lost Sunny now, he might not be able to find him again.

Freddie stopped just before the corner of the menagerie tent and peeped around it. Sunny was nowhere in sight. Freddie walked around the corner and stared down the empty path. Where had Sunny gone? Freddie was almost ready to give up and go back to the others when he saw the canvas flap of the tent entrance stir in the breeze.

He crept up to the entrance and listened hard. Nothing. He slipped inside. A long, gloomy hallway stretched out in front of him. The ceiling was canvas, but the walls on either side were made of thick planks. The heavy doors had steel bars on them. The place felt like a jail.

The hallway was empty. If Sunny had come in here, Freddie thought, he must have gone through one of the doors. But which one?

Freddie tiptoed down the hallway, stopping every few steps to listen. He was starting to wish that he hadn't run off on his own, that he had brought Nan and Flossie with him. It wasn't too late. All he had to do was turn around and—

The next door on the left was not closed all the way. He crept up to it and slowly, carefully, pushed it open. The room on the other side of the door was dark and silent. He pushed the door a little more.

Suddenly a hand shot out of the darkness and closed over his wrist. Freddie went flying forward, then fell to the floor. A moment later the door slammed.

He sat up and rubbed his knee. The floor seemed to be covered with straw, but the fall had hurt even so. Finally Freddie stood up, found the wall, and felt for the door. He tugged at the handle, but it didn't budge. He was locked in.

He put his ear to the door and listened. All at once he felt as if someone had touched an ice cube to the back of his neck.

He was not alone in the room. Something had just moved, behind him in the darkness. He could hear it breathing. And whatever it was, it sounded very, *very* big.

7

Magic Max Gets Mad

Freddie stood with his back to the wall and thought frantically. What could he do? He was trapped. If he tried to force the door open, the noise might attract whatever was in the room with him. And if he tried to find another way out in the darkness, he might even trip over the animal.

The straw rustled as the animal shifted its position again. At that moment, the lights came on. Freddie blinked and stared. There, almost close enough to touch, was a big gray elephant. It was lying on its side with its eyes closed. It looked nearly as big as a moving van.

Freddie glanced quickly around the room, but he didn't see any other doors. When he looked back at the elephant, its eyes were open, and it was looking straight at him. A moment later it rolled over onto its feet and started to stand up.

"Help!" Freddie yelled. "Get me out of here!"

The elephant took one step toward him, then another. Freddie tried to back away, but there was nowhere to go. The elephant lifted its trunk and reached for him.

"Help!" Freddie shouted again. The end of the elephant's trunk was only inches from his face. He turned away and shut his eyes tightly. Suddenly he felt something touching his chest. It tickled.

"Ranee, stop that!"

Freddie opened his eyes. Sarah was standing in the open doorway. Nan and Flossie were right behind her, staring over her shoulder. The elephant's trunk was slithering into Freddie's shirt pocket!

"Stop it," Sarah repeated. She pushed the elephant's trunk away. The elephant gave a loud snort and took a step backward. "She was just looking for peanuts," Sarah explained. "Her trainers usually keep a few in their pockets. How come the door was latched on the outside?"

"Somebody shut me in," Freddie said. He looked up at the elephant. It didn't look nearly as fierce as it had a few moments before. "I'm sorry, Ranee," he continued. "I'll try and bring you some peanuts later, okay?"

The elephant bobbed its head up and down, as if it understood him. Freddie stepped out into the hallway and took a deep breath.

Sarah shut the door behind her, then said, "Who shut you up in Ranee's enclosure? You could have gotten hurt."

"I didn't see his face," Freddie replied, "but whoever it was, I'll recognize his hand and his wristwatch. I'll bet it was Sunny."

"We're going to tell Max about this," said Sarah. She sounded really mad.

They found the circus owner in the office trailer, already wearing his ringmaster's costume. When he heard Freddie's story, his face turned almost as red as his coat.

"Bob," he said, looking over his shoulder, "go find Sunny. I want to see him right now!"

Max paced up and down, muttering to himself. Finally Bob reappeared. Sunny was right behind him.

Freddie glanced at the clown's hand and caught his breath. He was sure he recognized it. He looked up at Max and nodded.

"What's the idea," Max said, "of locking a little kid in the elephant pen?"

"What are you talking about?" Sunny replied.

Freddie, stung by being called a little kid, spoke up. "I saw your hand," he said, "and that watch you're wearing. I know it was you."

Sunny glared at him, then at Max. "Are you going to take that brat's word over mine?" he demanded.

"You bet I am," the circus owner said. "And don't call people names. Once and for all, Sunny, why did you shut the kid in Ranee's pen?"

The clown looked around at the circle of faces, then stared at the ground. "It was just a joke," he said in a low voice. "He was snooping around and bothering me. I thought I'd teach him a lesson. I knew Ranee wouldn't hurt him."

"Not on purpose," Max said. "But what if there'd been an accident? You know that would have been the end for the show, don't you? But maybe you don't care."

"It was just a joke," Sunny repeated.

Max's face was turning red again. "Well, let me tell you something. Anybody who thinks that scaring the daylights out of a kid is a joke will never be a good clown. Never! And the Magic Max Circus doesn't have any room for

bad clowns. Think about it, Sunny. Think very hard."

Sunny looked as if he wanted to answer the circus owner. Finally, though, he turned around and left the trailer without a word.

"I wonder," Nan said once the door was shut. "Do you think that falling trapeze last night was supposed to be a joke, too?"

Max turned on her. "Now, hold on, young lady," he said. "I don't like what Sunny did, not at all. But your brother wasn't really in any danger."

"*I* didn't know that," Freddie protested.

"Maybe not, but it's true. That trapeze incident, though, that's another story. To do something like that on purpose would be very serious. And you'd better think twice before you go around accusing somebody of a crime."

Bert was feeling frustrated. For over an hour he had been wandering around the fairgrounds. He had watched the performers and crew getting ready for the afternoon show. He had talked to some of them, too—the seal trainer and the sharpshooter and a member of the trapeze act, among others.

They all agreed that Togo was one of the best-liked people in the troupe. The idea that he was a crook, they said, was too ridiculous to talk about.

But someone had committed those burglaries. Lieutenant Pike hadn't made them up. He hadn't made up that sack full of loot in Togo's trailer, either. Someone—the burglar—had left it there. But why? To frame Togo? Or simply to hide the loot? Why hide it in someone else's quarters, where it might be found at any time?

Bert shook his head. At this point they had too many questions and not enough answers.

He had been too busy thinking to notice where he was going. Now he glanced around. This looked like the place where they had first met Sarah. One of the trailers farther down the row must be Togo's.

Bert frowned. A man had just come out of a trailer and was walking in his direction. Bert couldn't be completely sure at this distance, but he thought the man had come from Togo's trailer. Could this be their burglar, come back to look for his booty?

The man didn't *look* much like a burglar. He had a trim mustache and was wearing aviator sunglasses, a dark gray business suit, and well-shined shoes. In his left hand was a leather briefcase.

The man noticed Bert looking at him and

seemed to hesitate for a moment. Then he walked past, very quickly. Bert turned and stared after him.

In spite of the suit and tie and the sunglasses and the mustache, Bert was positive that he had recognized the man. It was Togo.

But why was he in disguise? And where was he going, so shortly before showtime?

8

The Funny-Face Clue

Bert stared as Togo disappeared around a corner, then set out at a run. He had to follow Togo and see where he went. The solution to the case might depend on it.

Bert's bicycle was still in the rack near the entrance to the big top. He was unlocking it when he heard Flossie calling his name.

"Where were you?" she said, running up to him. "I came looking for you. Where are you going?"

"No time to talk," Bert replied. "I'm shadowing somebody."

"Who is it? Can I help?"

"Sure, come on, but speed it up."

As she was taking her bike out of the rack, a pedal got caught in the spokes of Nan's front wheel. Bert ground his teeth and reminded himself to count to ten. Finally Flossie managed to free the pedal.

When they reached the street, the man in the sunglasses was nowhere around.

"I'm sorry," Flossie said. "It's all my fault we lost him."

Bert had just been thinking the same thing, but she sounded so upset that he said, "No, it's not. I shouldn't have let him get out of sight in the first place."

"What do we do now?"

Bert thought for a moment. "Let's check the schedule at the bus stop," he said. "If one left in the last few minutes, he might have caught it. But if not, he's probably still in the area."

The most recent bus had left over twenty minutes earlier. "Okay," Bert said, hopeful again. "Search party!"

Down one street they rode, then up the next. At each corner they paused just long enough for a careful look in each direction, then raced to the next corner.

After almost half an hour of searching, they were discouraged and out of breath.

"Maybe he took a taxi," Flossie said.

"Or somebody met him in a car," Bert replied. "Come on, we might as well go back."

They turned in the direction of the fair-grounds and started to pedal. Suddenly Bert swerved and exclaimed, "Look! That white house on the left!"

The front door of the house had just opened and a man was stepping out. A man with a mustache and wearing sunglasses and carrying a briefcase.

"Quick, over here!" said Bert. He led Flossie behind a hedge on the other side of the street. They cautiously raised their heads to watch.

A woman with white hair was standing in the doorway, talking to the man. After a moment he reached into his jacket pocket and took out what looked like a big wad of money. The woman seemed to be protesting, but he put the wad in her hand and gave her a goodbye kiss.

"He's in an awful hurry," Bert whispered as the man started walking down the sidewalk.

"Who is he?" asked Flossie. "He looked sort of familiar, but I don't think I've seen him before. And who is that woman, and why did he give her all that money?"

Bert snorted. "If we want any answers, we'd better follow him. Come on—he's nearly out of sight already!"

The man walked quickly back to the fair-grounds and circled the big top to the back

area. By the time Flossie and Bert convinced the guard to let them past, he had vanished.

"Oh, no!" Flossie wailed. "Not again! I can't *bear* another long search!"

"We won't have to search for long," Bert replied. "Not if my hunch is right." He led the way to Togo's trailer and knocked on the door.

After a long pause, Togo opened it. His face was only half made up. "Hi, kids," he said. "Sorry I can't talk. I'm running late."

"Okay," Bert said. "We'll catch you later."

As Togo was shutting the door, Bert craned his neck to look around him. On a chair near the door was a gray business suit, tossed down in a hurry. And on the dressing table were a pair of aviator sunglasses and what looked like a fake mustache.

"*Why* do we have to go home?" Freddie demanded. "I want to stay for the matinee."

"There's the early show this evening," Nan pointed out. "Maybe you can talk Mom and Dad into letting you come back for it. Right now we need a conference. We have to talk about what we've learned so far and what it all means."

"And don't forget we all have chores to do," Bert added.

"Aw, come on," said Freddie. "We're on a case!"

Bert grinned. "You don't want anyone on *your* case, do you?"

They rode home and settled in the backyard. First Nan told about the faint scratches on the list of advance-ticket buyers. She explained why she thought she knew whom the burglar's next victim would be. Then Flossie and Bert told of following the disguised man on his mysterious errand.

"It was Togo," Bert concluded. "I know it was."

"And Bert saw the disguise afterward in his trailer," said Flossie. "That proves it."

"Huh," Freddie said with a look of disgust. "All *I* discovered this afternoon was that being trapped in the dark with an elephant is scary."

"Be fair," said Nan. "You're the one who noticed Sunny, and followed him, and identified him after he played that dirty trick on you. That's good detective work."

"Huh," Freddie repeated, but he looked a little happier. He pulled the three sponge balls from his pocket and started to juggle them.

Mrs. Bobbsey called from the window, "I'm baking some cookies for snacks, and I need some helpers. Who wants to run the mixer?"

A moment later, all four Bobbseys were racing across the yard for the back door.

After a delicious snack, the twins all gathered in the driveway before heading back to the circus.

"But why can't we come with you?" Flossie demanded.

Nan shook her head. "Look, I don't *know* there's going to be a burglary this evening. If I did, I'd call Lieutenant Pike and warn him. I just have a hunch, that's all. But I think Bert and I ought to check it out. We'll take a look, then meet you guys at the circus. Okay?"

"Well . . ." Flossie said slowly.

"Come on," Freddie said. "Togo's is one of the first acts. We don't want to miss him."

Nan and Bert rode with the younger twins most of the way to the fairgrounds, then turned off for what might be a rendezvous with a burglar.

The address Nan had copied down was a two-story house a few blocks from the fairgrounds. The twins hid their bikes behind some hedges, then found a hiding place under the neighbor's rose bushes. Nan and Bert settled down to wait and watch.

At a little after six-thirty, just as it was getting dark, two grown-ups and two children came out the back door, climbed into the station wagon in the driveway, and drove off.

Bert was starting to say something when Nan poked him in the ribs. A motorbike had just turned the corner and was putt-putting up the block. It swerved into the driveway and stopped just in back of the house. The rider was dressed all in black and was wearing a helmet with a dark visor. He looked around. For a long moment he seemed to stare straight at Bert and Nan. Then he vanished behind the house.

"We'd better call the cops," Bert whispered.

"Wait," Nan replied. "If we leave now, we might lose him for good."

It seemed to take forever, but finally the mysterious rider reappeared. He had what looked like a full pack on his back. After three or four tries, he started his motorbike and aimed it down the driveway.

"Come on!" Nan said. "This is our chance!"

The twins dashed to their bicycles and pedaled furiously after the motorbike. Luckily, the burglar's engine wasn't working very well. They almost managed to keep up with him. When he stopped for a red light, they even had to halt down the block to keep from being discovered.

"I knew it," said Bert. "He's heading for the fairgrounds!"

"We can't lose him now," Nan said as the light changed and the motorbike putted away. "Come on!"

As they came even with the midway, the rider glanced back once, then a second time. The motorbike speeded up.

"He spotted us!" Bert shouted.

Nan and he rode as hard and fast as they could, trying to overtake the burglar in the helmet. They were gaining on him as they neared the big top. Suddenly from the enormous tent came a roar of cheers and applause. The Bobbseys couldn't help looking over that way. When they looked back, the motorbike was heading straight for the performers' entrance to the tent. An instant later the bike and its rider had vanished.

9

Thrills and Spills

A young guard—not Ben, who knew the twins—barred the entrance. "Sorry, kids," he said. "No one's allowed in this way."

"But we're working for Max," Bert protested.

"We're the Bobbseys," added Nan. "Check your list, *please!*" She tried to look around him. Where was their burglar now?

"Sorry," the guard repeated. "Rules are rules."

"But . . ." Twenty feet away, inside the tent, a half-dozen horses clustered together. Nan searched the area and saw a familiar figure. "Sarah," she called out. "Sarah!"

Sarah waved, then strolled over to tell the

guard the Bobbseys were okay. A few moments later, Freddie and Flossie came over, too.

"No time to explain," Nan said. "Did any of you see a man in black on a motorbike?"

"There's a motorbike over near the animal cages," Freddie said.

Bert studied it. "It looks like the one," he said, "but where's the rider?"

"Somebody wearing a helmet ran past me—to the dressing rooms, I think," Sarah said. "I thought he might have hurt himself. He looked like he was limping. Hey, I'd better go or I'll be late for my number."

Nan looked around. The show was in full swing. In the near ring, eight acrobats were balancing on the shoulders of a ninth, who was riding a bicycle in circles. In the far ring, a team of tumblers with a springboard were doing back flips and somersaults in midair. And in the center ring, Togo was juggling a whirl of Indian clubs while flipping a hat from his head to his outstretched foot and back again.

Closer at hand, Lieutenant Pike and two uniformed officers were standing near the entrance to the arena. It seemed to Nan that all three were carefully watching Togo. Did they believe they had enough evidence to arrest him again? They'd be proved wrong—since Togo was juggling in the center ring, he couldn't possibly be the mysterious burglar.

"We'd better split up," Bert said. "He might have circled around under the stands. You and Freddie go left, and Flossie and I will go right."

"Right," Nan replied. "Let's go!"

She and Freddie started off down the corridor between the canvas outer wall of the big tent and an ordinary picket fence that blocked off a storage area for lion cages, tumblers' ladders, and trick motorcycles. The dressing rooms turned out to be five motor homes parked nose to tail under the bleachers.

"What now?" Freddie asked in a low voice. "Maybe he's hiding in one of them."

"Let's go to the far end and work our way back," Nan said softly. She led the way, looking carefully into the shadows, then jumped as something moved. A moment later she heard a faint bleat. It was a goat. She remembered seeing it, or one just like it, balancing on a beach ball during the show the day before.

"You scared me," she whispered to the goat.

"Me, too," said Freddie.

The goat bleated again, louder.

"Shhh!"

Nan and Freddie reached the last dressing room. Nan carefully tried the door. It was locked. Freddie peered in one of the windows. "It's all dark," he reported.

"Let's try the next one," Nan said.

This time the door opened easily. They checked the closets and the tiny washroom. Freddie even got down on the floor to look under the couch. There was no trace of their black-clad burglar.

"We don't even know that he came this way," Freddie said. "Sarah wasn't sure about that."

"There aren't too many places he could have gone," Nan replied. "We'd better cover them all."

She started out the door of the trailer, then stopped so suddenly that Freddie bumped into her.

"There he is," she whispered. "That's him!"

The man in black had just come out of the first trailer and was walking quickly up the corridor. He was no longer carrying a backpack. Had he just hidden his loot in the trailer?

"Come on, we've got him now!" Nan began to run on tiptoe after the retreating burglar. Freddie was right behind her. The man in black looked over his shoulder, then broke into a limping run.

"He can't get away," Freddie cried, pouring on speed.

At that moment, though, the man made a spectacular leap over the picket fence onto the saddle of one of the parked motorcycles. The engine started with a roar. Gravel sprayed as the motorcycle flew down the narrow corridor toward the performers' entrance. In another second the burglar would get away for good.

"Stop him!" Nan screamed. "Stop him!"

The crowd near the arena entrance turned to look. Bert and Flossie came running from the other direction. At almost the last moment, Lieutenant Pike and one of his officers dashed over to block the exit.

For a moment it looked as if the rider were going to run them down. At the last instant he swerved wildly. The motorcycle leaned far over, almost falling, then recovered. It steered around the waiting horses and cleared the entrance to the arena.

Nan had a painful stitch in her side, and her lungs felt as though they were going to burst, but she kept running. Behind her, Flossie tried to keep up. Bert drew closer. Suddenly Sarah, on horseback, galloped past her. A few seconds later Freddie rode by on his bicycle, but the man on the motorcycle was far ahead of all of them.

They were nearly halfway around the arena but Nan couldn't run any farther. She stopped to catch her breath, and Bert skidded to a halt next to her.

"Let's try to block him off," he shouted. He pointed to two stands, like giant footstools, that the seals had been sitting on a few minutes earlier. "Quick!"

The people in the audience were laughing and clapping. They thought the wild chase was part of the show. Nan and Bert each grabbed one of the hard rubber stands and carried it to the cinder track on the far side of the arena. The stands weren't wide enough to completely block the way, but they narrowed it a lot.

"Look out!" Nan shouted. They jumped aside as the motorcycle roared down on them.

The cheers of the audience changed to screams. The cyclist swerved left, then right, but he couldn't turn sharply enough to dodge the two obstacles. Suddenly the motorcycle was sliding sideways down the track. The engine howled, and a choking cloud of dust rose almost to the roof of the tent.

The motorcycle slammed into the heavy barrier around the arena. The engine died. The audience fell silent.

Nan stared through the curtain of dust. The rider in black had been thrown from the motorcycle when it crashed. He was lying very still.

10

The Grand
Finale

Two police officers rushed up and unstrapped the rider's helmet. Bert caught Nan's eye and nodded. "It's Max's assistant, Bob Sawyer," he said.

"Nan figured it out," Flossie said as she and Freddie ran up to join Bert and Nan.

"I don't care," said Freddie. "I still think Sunny was a better suspect. A meaner one, anyway."

The police officers helped the dazed Sawyer onto a stretcher, then the first-aid crew carried him away. The Bobbseys followed close behind.

As they neared the exit, Sarah and her family rode into the arena. Sarah was doing a headstand on her saddle, and her father was riding two horses at once, one foot on each one. The audience gave them a big round of applause.

Max and Togo were standing just offstage. Max was wiping his forehead with a white handkerchief.

"Bob," he said when the first-aid crew set down the stretcher. "Bob, why did you do it?"

"I'm sorry, Max," his assistant said. "You might as well know—I've been stealing from the show for weeks now. I needed the money for Cindy's hospital bills."

"Why didn't you tell me?" Max said.

"Or me?" asked Togo. "We would have found the money somehow."

Bob shook his head. "I couldn't ask you for any more. Even what I took from the box office wasn't enough. That's when I got the idea of breaking into houses while their owners were watching the circus."

Bert pushed forward in the little crowd around the stretcher. "Why did you try to throw the blame on Togo?" he demanded.

"I never meant to." Bob sighed. "I like Togo. But I had to borrow his car because my motorbike broke down. I never thought anyone would notice the car and report it to the cops."

"And the stolen goods in Togo's trailer?" asked Nan. "What about that?"

"I had to put the stuff somewhere. I couldn't keep it in the dorm with me, could I? After the cops took him away, I went back to get whatever they hadn't found. I didn't want to leave any more evidence against him. I nearly got caught, too."

"So it *was* you in the closet," Bert exclaimed. "I thought so!"

"Why?" asked Togo.

"The footprints outside the window of Togo's trailer," Bert replied.

"One was a lot deeper than the other," Flossie said.

Freddie added, "That was because of Bob's limp."

"That's pretty clever," Max said.

Bob sighed again and said, "I still don't understand how you kids found me out."

Nan explained about the list of names she had spotted in the office. "That's how we figured out where you were going to be."

Bob shook his head. "I nearly didn't go this evening," he said. "And if I hadn't, you never would have caught me."

"Oh, yes, we would," Freddie began. Bert shushed him.

Red lights flashed as an ambulance backed up to the entrance. Two medics picked up the stretcher and placed Bob in the ambulance. A police officer climbed into the ambulance next to him.

Max went over as the medic started to close the ambulance door. "Bob?" he said. "I'll see about a lawyer first thing in the morning. And about Cindy—don't worry, she'll be taken care of."

Sarah nudged Nan. "What did I tell you?" she whispered. "Just like one big family."

"What are you doing here?" Nan replied as the ambulance roared toward the road. "I thought you were out there performing."

"I made my exit a little early. I just had to know what was going on out here." She giggled. "I hope Mom and Dad aren't mad at me."

"Because you cut the act short, you mean?"

"No. Because I got here before they did!"

Bert cleared his throat. "There's one thing I still don't understand," he said. "Togo, why did you go off in disguise this afternoon? And where did you go?"

The clown rolled his eyes. "I *thought* you recognized me," he said.

"We followed you, too," said Flossie. "Who was that lady you were talking to?"

Togo looked around the circle of faces. "I have a confession to make," he began.

Lieutenant Pike elbowed his way to the front. "A confession?" he said.

"Oh, not that kind," Togo replied. "The fact is, I was visiting my mother. She's lived here in Lakeport for a couple of years."

"Oh," Bert said. "But why the disguise?"

Togo hung his head. "My mother doesn't know I'm a clown. And she won't like it when she finds out. She doesn't think clowning is dignified or respectable."

"That's silly," Flossie said, moving closer to him. "Clowns are wonderful. And you're especially wonderful."

"Why, thank you, Flossie. I like being a clown. I like making people laugh and feel happy. I wouldn't want to do anything else. But I never dared tell my mother what I did. She still thinks I'm a dentist, like my older brother."

"And that's why you tried to hide where you were going this afternoon," Nan said.

"That's right. I've been working up my nerve to tell her the truth, and I didn't want her to find out some other way first."

"Well, *I* think she'll be really proud," Freddie declared. "She ought to be. You're one of the greatest clowns in the world!"

Togo reached out and put his hands on Fred-

die's and Flossie's shoulders. "I owe you Bobbseys a lot," he said. "And I don't mean for all
those nice compliments, either. You cleared my
name and saved the Magic Max Circus from
ruin. And I think I know just the reward you
deserve. . . ."

It was eight o'clock, Tuesday evening—
showtime once again at the Magic Max Circus.
Backstage, Freddie Bobbsey tugged at the giant
bowtie around his neck. "I feel sick," he said.

Nan was busy adjusting the jewel-studded
gold bracelet on her upper arm. "Don't be
silly," she said. "You'll be terrific."

"But what if I drop the balls?"

Bert straightened his red-and-green turban.
"You won't," he said. "And if you do, Togo
will make it look like you did it on purpose. I
think this thing is going to fall off my head."

"Ta-dah!" said Flossie. She twirled around to
show off her leopard-print leotard and satiny
cape.

"You look terrific."

Sarah rode up on her horse and looked them
over. "You'll do," she said finally, then grinned.
"I hope somebody's taking pictures."

Max walked over, every inch a ringmaster.
"Are you ready, kids?" he asked. "Just re-

member, everybody in the show is going to be watching out for you. Whatever happens, you're out there to have a good time. And here's your ride now!"

Freddie jumped as a long gray trunk snuffled at his neck. "Stop that, Ranee!" he said.

"All aboard," Ali, the elephant trainer, said. He tapped Ranee on the neck, and she knelt down. Max helped Flossie, Nan, and Bert onto the little platform strapped to the elephant's back. Another tap, and the elephant stood up.

"Eek," said Flossie. "It's awfully far up, isn't it?"

Bert chuckled. "It's a long way down, too," he teased.

Freddie, still on the ground, said, "I feel sick." But he took out his juggling balls and started to practice.

A flourish from the brass band, and the grand entrance parade began. Sarah and her family led the way on horseback, carrying colorful banners, followed by a group of acrobats. Next came two clowns who juggled as they marched. One of them was pretty small, but they both drew big cheers from the crowd.

Ranee was next. Each of the three performers riding the elephant waved to the audience with one hand. With the other they clung to the rail of the platform. But even if they seemed a little unsure of themselves, they all wore wide grins that drew laughter and cheers from the spectators.

The cheers were loudest as the procession passed one of the boxes. Richard and Mary Bobbsey were there, and so were a dozen friends of the twins. All of them had been invited as guests of the owner for a very special performance of the Magic Max Circus—starring, for one night only, the Bobbsey twins.